As for me, I've made lots of friends in London . . .

Mademoiselle Dubois, the cyclist - she gives me a ride every morning . . .

Mademoiselle Dubois

Dr Jafri who is always forgetting his keys . . .

Dr Jafri

Mrs Kitts and Feathers

and Mrs Kitts, who runs the newspaper kiosk with her parrot, Feathers.

Not forgetting, of course, my dear old friend, Mr Gruber, who runs Gruber's Antiques. People are awfully kind to me. I do hope if you could see me you'd be pleased.

Lots of love from, Padingtun

Mr Gruber

Paddington was going to Mr Gruber's shop that very day to look for the perfect present for his Aunt Lucy, who would be celebrating her hundredth birthday that year!

"I've just had a visit from Madame Kozlova," Mr Gruber told Paddington. "She runs the steam fair that's come to town. She was having a clear-out and found a trunk of old memory-bilia that she wants me to sell for her."

Rummaging through the trunk, Paddington found a beautiful pop-up book all about London. Apparently, it was handmade by Madame Kozlova's great-grandmother. It wasn't cheap to buy...but it was perfect.

"Aunt Lucy always dreamed of coming to London," Paddington said, excitedly. "If she saw this, it would be as if she were finally here. I'm going to get a job and buy that book!"

PADDINGTON™ 2
The Movie Storybook

1 3 5 7 9 10 8 6 4 2
ISBN: 978-0-00-825448-3
First published in paperback in Great Britain by HarperCollins Children's Books in 2017

Written by Stella Gurney, designed by Claire Yeo

Based on the Paddington novels written and created by Michael Bond
PADDINGTON™ and PADDINGTON BEAR™
© Paddington and Company Limited/STUDIOCANAL S.A.S. 2017

It was the height of summer in London, as Paddington Bear sat down to write his fortnightly letter to his beloved Aunt Lucy in Peru.

Dear Aunt Lucy,

It's been a very busy summer in Windsor Gardens.

Mrs Brown has decided to swim the English Channel. She trains every morning in the lake in Hyde Park.

Mrs Brown

Judy has found an old printing press at school, and I've been helping her set up her own newspaper.

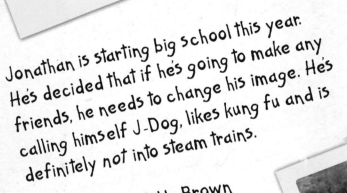

Judy

Jonathan

Jonathan is starting big school this year. He's decided that if he's going to make any friends, he needs to change his image. He's calling himself J-Dog, likes kung fu and is definitely not into steam trains.

And Mr Brown? Mr Brown is having what Mrs Bird calls A Full-Blown Mid-Life Crisis, and has taken up a little-known form of yoga called 'Chakrabatics'. I'm sure he'll get better at it very soon.

Mr Brown

That evening, the Browns and Paddington visited Madame Kozlova's Steam Fair. It was being opened by the actor, Phoenix Buchanan, who was once very famous but now made dog food commercials. He also happened to be a neighbour of the Browns and one of Mr Brown's insurance clients.

Paddington told Phoenix all about the pop-up book he wanted to buy for his Aunt Lucy. Phoenix was extremely interested.

After a couple of false starts, Paddington found a job he was good at — window cleaning!

Before long, he had a jar full of money and realised that soon he'd have enough to buy Aunt Lucy the pop-up book for her birthday! He was so excited, he decided to go past Mr Gruber's shop on his way home to take another look at the book through the shop window. It was every bit as beautiful as Paddington remembered.

As he was admiring it, he heard the tinkling of broken glass from the side of the shop. Someone was climbing in through Mr Gruber's window!

"Stop, thief!"
cried Paddington.

"Lawks!" the intruder gasped, hastily pulling himself inside. Paddington climbed in the window after him, following the thief as he burst out again through the front door.

The burglar alarm began to shriek as Paddington glanced at the glass case. The pop-up book was gone!

Paddington gave chase after the thief . . .
but as he raced out of the shop, the police
arrived just behind him.

"Robbery in progress at Gruber's Antiques. Suspect is . . . a small bear in a duffle coat and a red hat."

Paddington ran and ran as fast as he could.
At last he caught up with the burglar.

"Al-wight," said the thief. "You got me."

And with that he disappeared,
in a puff of smoke . . .

. . . just as the police arrived.

"Put your, um . . . paws in the air," demanded the policewoman.

"But *I'm* not the thief," insisted Paddington. "I was *chasing* the thief! And then he . . . "

"What? Disappeared in a puff of smoke?" she said, sarcastically.

"Well . . . yes," answered poor Paddington, helplessly.

The Browns were horrified when Paddington was brought home by the police.

"There must be some mistake," insisted Mr Brown.

"No mistake, sir," said the policeman shaking his head. "Caught red-handed robbing Gruber's Antiques."

"Well, well, well," called Mr Curry, the Browns' mean-spirited neighbour. "The truth is out. We opened our hearts and doors to that bear — well, you did. And all along, he was robbing you blind. I hate to say I told you so, but I definitely did tell you so!"

Paddington's neighbours and friends muttered anxiously amongst themselves as the confused bear was driven away in the back of a police van.

Except for one neighbour, who sat in a secret room in his attic nearby, removing his disguise. It would appear that the thief was in fact none other than . . .

PHOENIX BUCHANAN!

As he took off his make-up, Phoenix revealed his wicked plan.

"I will return to glory," he declared, "with the greatest one-man show the West End has ever seen! It'll cost a fortune, but if I'm right, a fortune's exactly what this pop-up book will unlock. All we need to do . . ." he muttered, peering at a pop-up of the Tower of London,

" . . . is follow the clues in Madame Kozlova's book . . . "

The next day, Paddington's case was heard in court.
Mr Gruber was the first on the witness stand.

"Tell me, Mr Gruber," asked the lawyer, disapprovingly, "did Paddington Brown show an interest in the pop-up book before it was stolen?"

"Oh yes," Mr Gruber nodded. "Paddington loved the book. He had his heart set on it."

"You discussed how expensive it was?" she asked.

"Yes, but he was earning the money! I refuse to believe that Paddington would ever burglarise my shop."

Finally, Phoenix Buchanan was called to the stand.

"Mr Buchanan, you were an eyewitness to the events?"

"Quite so. I was up late writing my forthcoming one-man show when I heard a hullabaloo. That's when I saw Paddington rushing down the street."

"Mrs Brown drew this based on the bear's description of the man he claims he was chasing. Did you see him?" asked the lawyer.

"Handsome devil, isn't he? Strong cheekbones, noble forehead, dazzling eyes . . ."

"But did you see him?"

"Alas, I did not."

It was no good. The judge banged his gavel.

"Paddington Brown. I hereby sentence you to ten years for grand theft."

Dear Aunt Lucy,

A great deal has happened since I last wrote. I'm afraid there's been a bit of a mix-up and I've had to leave Windsor Gardens and move . . . somewhere else.

It's not quite as charming as the Browns' house but it's not all bad. It's a period property. In fact, it's one of the most substantial Victorian buildings in London – and the security arrangements are second to none.

The Browns have promised to do all they can to bring me home. I can't wait to see them – they're bound to have sorted it all out. In the meantime, I think I'll try to get to know the neighbours.

Your loving nephew,

Padingtun

Meanwhile, the Browns and Mrs Bird were desperate to prove Paddington's innocence.

HAVE YOU SEEN **THIS MAN?**

PHONE 0207 946 0329

HAVE YOU SEEN **THIS MAN?**

PHONE 0207 946 0329

Judy printed a special edition of her paper, and Jonathan stuck up posters all over the neighbourhood.

"I think there's something fishy about this whole business," sighed Mrs Brown. "I mean – of all the treasures why did the thief only take the pop-up book?"

"He probably didn't know much about antiques," shrugged Mr Brown. "He hardly looks the sort."

"Maybe. Or maybe he knows something about the pop-up book that we don't . . ."

Unfortunately, Paddington's attempts to get on with his fellow prisoners didn't go as well as he'd hoped, and when he accidentally put a red sock in with the prison laundry and dyed everyone's uniforms pink, he became positively unpopular.

"Afternoon, chaps," he said as he sat down to eat with his fellow inmates. "If you ask me, the pink really brightens things up."

Seeing their expressions, Paddington hastily changed the subject, and asked what exactly was the slop they all had in their bowls?

Nobody knew, and nor did anyone dare ask Knuckles, the prison chef.

"Tell you what, son," said a prisoner called T-Bone. "You get Knuckles to change the menu, and we might all forgive you for making us look like a bunch of pink flamingos ..."

Paddington couldn't help feeling that T-Bone's smile was a little threatening, but reminding himself of Aunt Lucy's saying: "If you look for the good in people, you'll find it," he approached the prison chef for a friendly chat about his food ...

. . . although he quickly realised he may have misjudged the situation somewhat.

As Paddington looked up at Knuckles's furious face he had a flash of inspiration. He removed the emergency sandwich from beneath his hat and shoved it into Knuckles's mouth.

"What is it?" asked Knuckles.

"It's marmalade!"
Paddington stammered.

"Marm-a-lade?" breathed Knuckles, in wonder. "You know how to make this?"

From that moment on Paddington was under Knuckles's protection. There was just one condition: Paddington was to teach him everything he knew about making marmalade.

Back at Windsor Gardens, Mrs Brown couldn't shake the feeling that the thief knew something important about the pop-up book. So the Browns and Mrs Bird paid a visit to the steam fair to see Madame Kozlova to find out more about it.

And what a story Madame Kozlova had to tell . . .

"My great-grandmother, who started this fair, was the greatest show-woman of her generation," she told them. "She could tame lions, breathe fire and swallow swords. But she was most famous for her trapeze act. They called her The Flying Swan.

Wherever she went she was showered with gifts, and she made a fortune. But where there is a fortune ... there is also jealousy.

The magician, a brilliant but selfish man, wanted her fortune for himself, so one night he cut the ropes of her trapeze. And The Flying Swan ... became the dying swan. As she lay there, he pretended to help her, but in fact stole a key she kept on a chain around her neck.

The magician went to her caravan and opened her strongbox with the key. But instead of her treasure, all he found was her handmade pop-up book of London.

The police came after him – they had him cornered. But just as they were about to arrest him, the magician vanished in a puff of smoke ... and was never heard of again."

"There's got to be something special about that pop-up book,"
Mrs Brown said to Mr Brown, later that evening. "Madame Kozlova
said there are twelve different landmarks in it. I wonder whether
they're ... I don't know ... *clues?*"

"Clues?" scoffed Mr Brown.

"To where she hid her fortune," exclaimed Mrs Brown, warming to her theme.
"And *that's* why the thief stole it from Mr Gruber!"

Mr Brown was not convinced, but Mrs Brown wouldn't be swayed. "I think
there's more to him than meets the eye," she said. "I think he somehow knew
about the Kozlova fortune ...

... and is somewhere out there,
right now, trying to find it!"

As Mrs Brown pondered, outside St Paul's Cathedral, a group of nuns made their way slowly and gracefully up the steps and then began a reverent procession towards the altar. But as they went, one of them slipped away and sneaked up a winding staircase onto a balcony right in the magnificent dome: the Whispering Gallery. It was not a nun at all! It was Phoenix Buchanan!

There, he found what he was looking for – the letter 'A' carved into the marble base of an angel statue – just before he was spotted by a security guard. Phoenix ran, accidentally knocking the statue over the railings, but just managed to escape without being caught.

Across town, Knuckles woke Paddington for his secret marmalade-making lesson. He seemed to think, however, that this should involve Paddington doing all the work while he read his paper. Fortunately, after Paddington used one of his Hard Stares, Knuckles became much more cooperative. In fact, they worked rather well together.

Finally, the marmalade was ready.

"Well?" asked Knuckles, anxiously. "Is it any good?"

"There's only one way to find out . . ." answered Paddington.

The next morning, and much to Knuckles's surprise, his marmalade received a standing ovation. In fact, it went down so well that a few of the prisoners suggested other recipes they could make too.

"I can do strawberry panna cotta with a pomegranate glaze?" offered T-Bone.

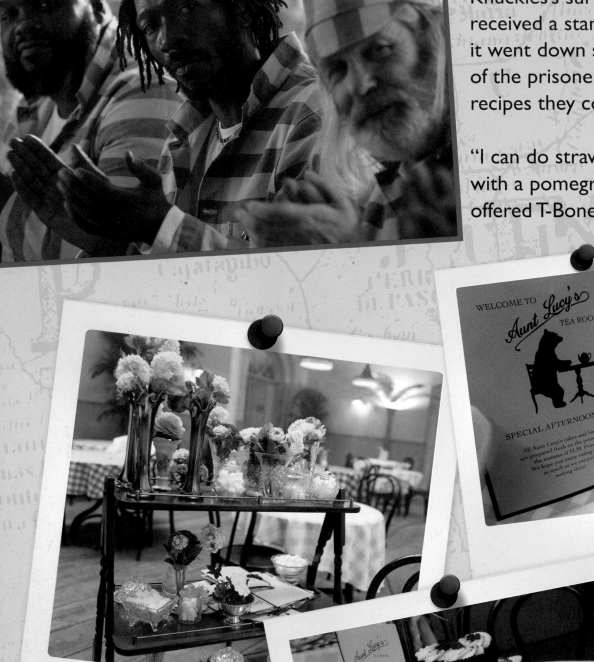

WELCOME TO
Aunt Lucy's
TEA ROOM

SPECIAL AFTERNOON TEA

All Aunt Lucy's cakes and biscuits are prepared fresh on the premises by the inmates of H.M. Prison. We hope you enjoy eating them as much as we enjoyed making them!

Before long, the canteen, and indeed
the whole prison, became a different
place altogether. And it was all thanks to
Paddington's influence . . . not to mention
Aunt Lucy's, who always said . . .

"If you're kind
and polite, the world
will be right."

Things were looking up in the prison but Paddington still couldn't wait for his monthly visit from the Browns. He felt sure they would have good news for him.

Delighted to see their little friend again, the Browns and Mrs Bird explained their new theory to him.

"Three shadowy individuals have been seen snooping around three London landmarks in the past week," said Mrs Brown.

"We think the thief is part of a criminal gang..." said Judy,

"...using the pop-up book as a treasure map!" finished Jonathan.

"So, do you know who they are?" asked Paddington.

There was a pause.

THE UN-USUAL SUSPECT

VITAL NEW CLUES IN PADDINGTON CASE POINT TO ORGANISED CR
LOCAL ILLUSTRATOR'S THEORY GATHERS MOMEN

"Not yet, dearie."
Mrs Bird shook her head.

"Maybe I should take a look," said Knuckles,
popping up with the rest of Paddington's new friends.
"If anyone can recognise a criminal, it's us."

But no one knew the men in the pictures. "I'm sorry to say it, kid," sighed
Knuckles, "but I think your family is barking up the wrong tree. A nun, a
beefeater and a king? Sounds more like a fancy dress party than a criminal gang."

"Then what are we going to do
now?" Paddington wondered.

No one knew the answer to this.

Time passed, and Paddington remained in prison. The Browns kept handing out leaflets, posters and newspapers, protesting his innocence.

Then one winter morning, as Mrs Brown dropped her latest bundle at Mrs Kitts's newspaper kiosk, she heard her name being called.

She turned to see Phoenix Buchanan standing at his balcony.

"Come on in!" he called. "I want to hear all about the investigation!"

But Phoenix wasn't really interested in the investigation.

Once he'd established that it hadn't got anywhere, he told Mrs Brown, "Well, I've got some news that might turn that little frown upside down. It looks like the funding is coming through for my one-man show! An evening of monologues and song – all my greatest creations back on stage. I call it, *The Phoenix Rises.*"

Mrs Brown sighed. "It seems so strange that Paddington's in prison but life carries on."

"I know, it must be hard to accept he won, the man with the dazzling blue eyes," Phoenix agreed.

"How do you know he had blue eyes?" she replied, sharply.

Phoenix faltered. "The man on the poster ... Your wonderful drawing!"

"It was a *pencil* sketch!"

Suddenly the penny dropped. He was the man! The thief! It was him —

PHOENIX BUCHANAN!

"PHOENIX BUCHANAN!"

snorted Mr Brown, when Mrs Brown explained her theory to the family later. "Let's just return to planet Earth for one moment. Phoenix Buchanan is a highly respected actor. He is not a petty thief. And might I remind you that you don't actually have any proof?"

Given that Phoenix was also a member of Mr Brown's insurance company's Platinum Club – and a Very Important Client – it was going to take a lot to change Mr Brown's mind.

But Mrs Bird had a plan . . .

. . . and she was not the only one.

Meanwhile, back in the prison . . .

"Psst! Paddington!"

Paddington scrambled up the central heating pipes in his cell
and opened up the air vent. "Knuckles?"

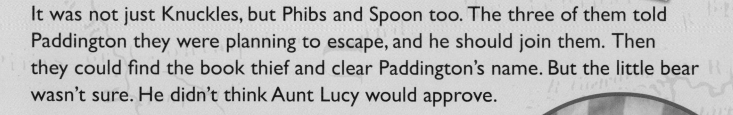

It was not just Knuckles, but Phibs and Spoon too. The three of them told
Paddington they were planning to escape, and he should join them. Then
they could find the book thief and clear Paddington's name. But the little bear
wasn't sure. He didn't think Aunt Lucy would approve.

"The Browns will come through for me,"
he assured his friends. "You'll see."

"You might not want to hear this, kid," said
Knuckles, gently, "but sooner or later your
family will give up on you."

"They'll miss one visit, then two," sighed Spoon.

"Before you know it,
they'll have abandoned
you altogether,"
Knuckles finished.

"You're wrong!"
exclaimed Paddington. "You're all wrong!
The Browns aren't like that!"

The next morning, Mrs Bird's plan was put into action: Mrs Brown hid inside a large hamper addressed to Phoenix's house.

Meanwhile, a fake phone call from Phoenix's agent, set up by Jonathan and Judy, lured him out of the building. Mrs Brown was free to search Phoenix's empty house.

Mr Brown, brushing his teeth in his pyjamas, spotted Mrs Brown through the bathroom window. "What the . . . !" he exclaimed, and hurried over to find out what his wife was up to.

But Mrs Brown had already found a note that looked interesting: *Saturday 06.35. Where All Your Dreams Come True,* and reluctantly Mr Brown joined her in looking for the pop-up book. They searched every room, and were just about ready to give up . . .

. . . when they found the secret attic.

"Look at all these costumes," exclaimed Mr Brown. "Good grief, he's a weirdo!"

Meanwhile, Phoenix realised he'd forgotten his cravat and turned back to get it . . .

Hearing him come in, Mr and Mrs Brown tried their best to hide but it was not long before Phoenix spotted Mr Brown's legs poking out from behind the sofa.

"Henry?" asked Phoenix in surprise.

"Phoenix," said Mr Brown, climbing out sheepishly.
He realised some explanation was needed.

"Umm. For our Platinum Club members, we perform an annual full-home inspection to verify your, ah, security arrangements."

It all seemed very unlikely, especially since Mr Brown was still in his pyjamas and Mrs Brown popped out from behind the curtain too, but Phoenix seemed to believe their story. He smiled as he showed them out . . .

... before sprinting up to his attic to check that the pop-up book was still where he had hidden it.

"That was close!" he sighed in relief.

"Hold your nerve," he told himself. "I've followed the clues all the way across London. At first, I thought they were just a bundle of letters from the alphabet, but then I realised they're musical notes ... and I know just where to play them!"

At the police station, the Browns reported what they had discovered, but without evidence, they were told it proved nothing. Crestfallen, they made their way out of the station, only to realise that they'd missed their visiting hour with Paddington!

Paddington waited and waited for the Browns, but no one came. He wondered whether his new friends were right – maybe his family *would* forget him eventually. Sadly, he decided the only thing for it was to escape with the prisoners who had promised to help him clear his name.

Everything went to plan, and before the night was out, Paddington found himself floating over London in a homemade hot-air balloon with his fellow fugitives.

Once they reached the East End docks, the prisoners brought the balloon down by an old factory on the river.

"There she is: our ticket out of here." Knuckles pointed to a seaplane waiting on the river. Paddington stopped short.

"But aren't we going to clear my name?"

Knuckles shrugged sheepishly. "Change of plan."

"We're leaving the country," grinned Spoon.

"But you said . . . you lied to me!" faltered Paddington.

"We've done you a favour! If we'd told you the truth you'd never have come!" protested Knuckles.

Paddington didn't want to leave the country. He wanted to clear his name and go home to the Browns. Betrayed and upset, he turned and ran.

Paddington spotted a phone box down a side alley. He dialled the Browns' number but the phone clicked to voicemail. Heartbroken, Paddington left a message and walked away, with no idea where he was going.

Then a magical thing happened: the phone rang.

Hardly daring to hope, the little bear ran to answer it.

"Paddington?" It was Mrs Brown!

"Yes, yes, it's Paddington!" he cried, relief flooding through him.

Joyfully, the family gathered round the phone, clamouring to tell Paddington how much they loved him; how they'd been up all night worrying.

"And we know who the thief is!" called Judy.

"IT'S PHOENIX BUCHANAN!"

"Mr Buchanan?" repeated Paddington, shocked.

"But he's disappeared into thin air!" said Mrs Bird. "We've been searching for him all night!"

"All we know is, that at 06:35 today, he'll be 'Where all your dreams come true!' Whatever that means." Mrs Brown told Paddington.

"I've seen that before," said Paddington slowly. "On the pop-up book and ... the organ at the steam fair!"

"That must be where Madame Kozlova hid her fortune!" cried Jonathan.

"The fair is leaving today . . ." gasped Judy.

"At 06:35!" Mrs Brown suddenly pieced it all together.

"There's still time!" said Mrs Bird looking at her watch.

"Paddington, get to the station," exclaimed Mr Brown. "If we can find Phoenix and get hold of that book, we can prove everything!"

But the Browns' car wouldn't start! And worse, Mr Curry had heard that Paddington had escaped and was standing in their way with a megaphone and his neighbourhood panic board set to Wild Hysteria.

"Get back to your homes!" cried Mr Curry.

But Paddington's neighbours took no notice.

"Go and bring Paddington home," smiled Dr Jafri, as he and the other neighbours gave the car a push-start.

Meanwhile, Paddington had arrived at the station before the Browns, managing to get on board the fair's steam train at the same time as a familiar-looking train guard.

The Browns and Mrs Bird arrived just a second too late. They chased after the fair's train as it pulled out of the station.

"We've got to catch up with that train!" cried Mrs Brown.

Jonathan spotted a magnificent old Pullman steam train on the other platform. "I've got an idea," he said.

Back on the moving train, the familiar-looking guard had removed his wig and was standing before Madame Kozlova's organ.

"Well, Grandfather," Phoenix addressed the carving of the wicked magician on the front. "The moment of truth."

Kneeling down, he played a series of twelve notes.

From the depths of the organ, a box of treasure arose. "Hello," breathed Phoenix. "Aren't you pretty."

Just then, he caught sight of Paddington hanging through the skylight, trying to grab hold of the pop-up book.

A thrilling chase followed, in which the Pullman, driven by Jonathan, pulled alongside the fair's train and Paddington tried to make his way across to safety.

60163

But before he could get across, Phoenix locked Paddington in the last coach of the train and set it loose! The others watched helplessly as Paddington's runaway carriage trundled down a broken track and tipped into the swirling river below.

Mrs Brown didn't hesitate. She dived in after Paddington.

She swam fast to the sinking carriage and pulled on the door. It opened a little but the chain was too strong.

Paddington was trapped!

Mrs Brown tugged and tugged at the door handle, but the chain wouldn't budge. Paddington and Mrs Brown looked at each other hopelessly through the crack in the door.

Suddenly, more hands were there, heaving at the door, and all at once the chain gave, the door burst open and Paddington was free!

Mrs Brown and Paddington burst from the surface of the water, gasping for air, and Knuckles, Spoon and Phibs emerged too, their seaplane bobbing on the water nearby.

"Knuckles!" spluttered Paddington in amazement. "What made you change your mind?"

"Can't make marmalade on my own now, can I?" the big man winked.

Paddington smiled happily.

At last, a very tired Paddington was back at 32 Windsor Gardens where he belonged. The police had realised there'd been a terrible mix-up, so they arrested Phoenix and Paddington was a free bear!

===

"You've been asleep for three days!" Jonathan told him when he opened his eyes.

"But that means it's too late to send Aunt Lucy a birthday present. She's going to wake up on her hundredth birthday and think I've forgotten her!" "Come with us," smiled Mr Brown.

Baffled, Paddington followed the Browns downstairs. The hallway was overflowing with people; it seemed the whole neighbourhood had come to wish him well.

"Oh, thank you, everyone! But what about Aunt Lucy?"

Just then, the doorbell rang.

"Why don't you go and answer it?" smiled Mrs Brown.

Standing on the doorstep, in the snow, was Aunt Lucy.

"Hello, Paddington, dear."

Paddington's face lit up with perfect joy.

"Happy birthday, Aunt Lucy!"

THE END